HANDA'S SURPRISE

EILEEN BROWNE

WALKER BOOKS
AND SUBSIDIARIES
LONDON · BOSTON · SYDNEY

Handa put seven delicious fruits in a basket
for her friend, Akeyo.

She will be surprised, thought Handa
as she set off for Akeyo's village.

I wonder which fruit she'll like best?

Will she like the soft yellow banana …

or the sweet-smelling guava?

Will she like the round juicy orange ...

or the ripe red mango?

Will she like the spiky-leaved pineapple ...

the creamy green avocado …

or the tangy purple passion-fruit?

Which fruit will Akeyo like best?

"Hello, Akeyo," said Handa. "I've brought you a surprise."

"Tangerines!" said Akeyo. "My favourite fruit."
"TANGERINES?" said Handa. "That *is* a surprise!"

monkey

ostrich

zebra

elephant

giraffe

antelope

parrot

goat